TABLE OF CONTENTS

THE PHANTOM TEACHER

by
Mike Anderson

1stBooks – rev. 03/028/01

Chapter 1
NOTES FROM THE OFFICE

"Hey, what did you do that for?" shouted the tall, skinny kid sitting next to me. Milk was dripping down his legs making a white puddle on Mrs. Koofer's kindergarten room's floor. The pencil thin kid picked up his carton. Soon I too had milk dripping from my head and running into the white pond on the floor. Mrs. Koofer sent us to see the principal who explained that milk was a drink not a toy. Stinky and I have been milk brothers ever since that first day of kindergarten.

1

Me? I'm Mike Chappel, the guy who wrote this book. I'm a regular sort of guy who's short and wears glasses. Last year I kicked the winning goal in the championship soccer game. The team Stinky and I are on won 3-2. If you want to see the game ball, it's in the corner of my room.

I do O.K. in school, although I do seem to get in more trouble than my parents and teachers like. It's not my fault though. Although my parents had hinted at it, who knew it was against the rules to pour milk on someone? No one ever said pouring milk was wrong. I've poured milk on lots of things, like cereal and oatmeal and my cat Fluffy.

Stinky and I knew all the basic rules of school: Don't hit, don't steal, don't say bad words, and don't flush your pencil down the toilet. But watch out for the hidden rules!

I discovered a lot of these rules when I made it into third grade. As a matter of fact, it's because of one of these secret rules that I had time to write this book. I ended up in Mr. Payson's office for a month or so with nothing else to do except write and clean bathrooms.

Second grade ended in a strange way. Mrs. Zehr, our teacher, lined us up and herded us into the hall.

"Where are we going?" whispered Stinky.

"If you two hadn't of been messing around you would know we're going to see the third grade teachers," said a girl named Amy.

We soon found out there were two of them: Ms. Timple and Mr. Thomas.

"I like her," whispered Stinky as he and I sat on the floor in front of them. "She looks nice." Ms. Timple was young and pretty. She was wearing a blue sweater with a teddy bear on the front.

I glanced at her; she looked a lot like my mom. Mr. Thomas was a man! I had never seen a man teacher that didn't teach gym. He was wearing a rumpled blue shirt and a tie with a fish on it. Both of them smiled and said hello when Mrs. Zehr introduced them.

"We understand that all of you will be in third grade next year," said Ms. Timple. Her voice was soft with just a touch of no nonsense in it.

Mr. Thomas cleared his throat and shoved his glasses up his nose, "Third grade is a

3

wonderful year, but it will be different than second. It will be a year of growing up and leaving little kid stuff behind." He glanced at Stinky and I.

A hand shot up next to Stinky, it was Amy's. "Will we have homework?"

Ms. Timple smiled, "Yes, you will." There was a collective moan.

"You also get to check out three books a week from the library and learn multiplication," said Mr. Thomas. We all listened, too nervous to goof around.

After Ms. Timple and Mr. Thomas had made their speeches, Mrs. Zehr lined us up to head back to the second grade room one last time. As we left the room, Mr. Thomas and Ms. Timple stood at the door and said good-bye.

As I passed, Ms. Timple said, "Isn't this the short kid with glasses who kicked the winning goal at the soccer championship?"

Mr. Thomas smiled, "It sure looks like him. Good shot!"

I nodded and headed out the door. I think that if I had grinned any bigger my ears would have fallen off. Even with homework, third grade was going to be as good as second!

As we headed down that hall, Stinky whispered, "I want Ms. Timple. I'm not so sure I want a man teacher."

I smiled, "Not me, I want Mr. Thomas." I liked Mr. Thomas because he **was** a guy. He was the only man teacher in the school.

Amy piped up, "My sister said they're both great teachers. We'll have fun with either one of them."

"I can't wait to have homework," said the kid next to Amy whose name was Tim.

Stinky rolled his eyes, "Yeah, homework will be a lot of fun."

A few minutes later Mrs. Zehr told us summer vacation had started and to please get out of her room.

Chapter 2
BEGINNINGS

I walked into the school without knowing whom I had for a teacher. My family had gone on vacation and just barely made it home for me to start third grade on time.

The secretary scanned a list on her desk, "You are in Mr. Thomas' room, fourth door on the left. Have a good year."

"See you after school!" said Dad as I headed down the hall.

I walked down the hall and went into the third door on the left. It was a bathroom. When

I stepped back into the hall, the secretary's voice echoed down the hall, "The next door!"

I pushed it open and stepped into the room.

"Come on in," said Mr. Thomas. "Have a seat anywhere you would like!"   .

I sat down next to Stinky and looked at the guy with whom I was going to spend the year.

Bearded Mr. Thomas didn't have much hair on top of his head. He was wearing the same fish tie he was wearing on the last day of school. I had heard from some kids that he was nice. Other kids had told me he was strict. Everyone agreed he was a little strange. Mr. Thomas seemed to be my kind of teacher.

While I liked the location of my desk, it wasn't exactly the right size. I must have been the only kid who didn't grow to third grade size over the summer. I had to stand to do my work.

"Mr. Thomas," I yelled, "I can barely see over the top of my desk."

"For the time being stand to do your work. You can sit down to rest. I'll see what I can do about getting your desk lowered tomorrow," he said.

Mr. Gregg, the janitor, paid me a visit on the second day of school. Mr. Gregg was a short, large man who always wore a brown work shirt, jeans, and a big leather belt with all sorts of things hanging from it. He called it his portable toolbox. It hung way down on his hips, pulling his pants down a bit too.

He clanked up to my desk. "You Mike Chappel? Mr. Thomas asked me to lower your desk. Better move!"

The janitor grabbed my desk and, with a grunt, flipped it over onto its top. I watched as my brand new, just opened box of 128 crayons went zipping across the floor. While I chased my Burnt Red crayon, the class watched Mr. Gregg take a hammer and a wretch from his belt and begin to twist and pound. After five minutes of making a lot of racket, he tightened a screw and flipped the desk back over. I looked up from underneath

Stinky's desk with a Lemon-Green crayon in my hand.

"You better not grow. I don't want to do this again," he growled.

I gathered the rest of my crayons and sat down. It felt great to put my elbows on the desk and have them lower than my chin.

As Mr. Thomas began to teach math, I wondered how I was supposed to stop growing. Third grade was going to be tough!

Chapter 3
SURROUNDED!

Things went pretty well for a week or so. I had stopped eating lunch to keep from growing, so I wasn't too worried about Mr. Gregg.

On the first day of school Mr. Thomas let us sit anywhere we wanted.

"I see no reason to change your seats unless you ask to be moved or I have a reason to move you." He also said something about making responsible choices, but I didn't catch what it was.

Stinky and I were finally able to sit next to each other for the first time since I dumped the milk on him in kindergarten. It was great!

"Hey, Stinky, ask Tim if he knows the answer to number 23," I whispered.

"He says the answer is 27 hot dogs. I got 35 hot dogs, what did you get?"

"I didn't get any hot dogs, my mom packed a peanut butter and jelly sandwich in my lunch."

Stinky burst out laughing and then quickly covered his mouth. We couldn't look at each other for the next couple of minutes or we'd break out in silent laughter.

"Hey, look at this!" Stinky handed a folded piece of paper over to me. I glanced at it and burst out laughing.

"I want to see!" said Tim.

I had no sooner handed the paper to Tim than a shadow fell across my desk.

"I want to see it after Tim," said Mr. Thomas.

"Uh, I'm not really all that interested in this, Mr. Thomas. You can have it before me." Tim smiled a weak little smile and gave the paper to Mr. Thomas.

"Thanks, Tim"

Stinky slid down into his seat and muttered, "Yeah, thanks, Tim."

Mr. Thomas walked to the front of the class and opened the paper. Much to Stinky's relief, Mr. Thomas smiled.

"This is an excellent drawing. However, I don't think a rocket would gain much from launching off of my bald head. It's a good drawing though, shall I keep it for parent conferences?"

Stinky cleared his throat, "Uh, my folks have already seen lots of my drawings. They probably don't need to see that one too."

"OK, but if I see another one of this quality, I will need to save it. Here you go." He handed the drawing to Tim. Who wasted no time in giving it back to Stinky.

"How about if I change a couple of seats around. Mr. Artist, why don't you sit over here? Mike, you sit here."

I gazed at Stinky who was now all the way over on the other side of the room between the Kluggy twins, Jeff and Jerry, two guys known for their lack of a sense of humor. They scowled at Stinky like an old piece of lunchmeat had been placed between them.

12

I was right in the middle of a bunch of girls. Surrounded!

Amy Fredricks poked me with her pencil, "You better be quiet, Mike Chappel. I don't want to get in trouble."

"So how do you like your new seat?" chuckled Stinky at lunch. "At least the Kluggy's are boys!"

"It's horrible," I moaned. "No one to talk to except girls." I flicked a piece of potato chip at him with my finger. "I tried to talk to them but they wouldn't talk to me! Mr. Thomas walked by, smiled, and told me that maybe I would learn to be quiet sitting there."

"I doubt that, but maybe you'll learn how to breathe in girl germs without passing out."

Chapter 4
A DATE?

Two days after Stinky and I got new seats in class, I decided talking to a girl was easier than not talking at all. Who knows, maybe girls were actually interesting. Anyway, Amy Fredricks is kind of cute for a girl. She has this long, black hair that goes all the way to her shoulders. I like to pull it when she's in front of me in line. She doesn't seem to enjoy it as much as I do.

I twisted in my seat, "Hey, can I borrow that neat little elephant pencil sharpener?" I whispered.

She looked at me, frowned, shook her head, and whispered a little too loudly, "No!"

When I turned back around, Mr. Thomas was staring straight at me. Then, loud enough for the whole class to hear, he said, "Mike, I know Amy's kind of cute, but please don't ask her out on a date in my class."

I mumbled, "I just wanted to borrow her pencil sharpener."

I heard Stinky start to laugh, quickly followed by the rest of the class. Nobody must have been listening when Mr. Thomas had been talking about self-control. Stinky was laughing so hard he almost fell out of his chair. The Kluggy twins, who never seemed to smile, were even chuckling softly to themselves.

"Really, all I wanted was her pencil sharpener. Honest! I didn't ask her for a date, I'm too young to date!"

No one could hear me over the laughter. Amy and I turned a deep red. I knew Amy would never talk to me again. I also knew I would never, ever, talk to another girl in class.

The next day I got Mom to buy me a pencil sharpener. It was two months before Amy and I got everyone to believe we didn't like each other.

Chapter 5
"LISTEN; DO, WAH, DO"

I settled down quite a bit after that. I didn't dare talk to any of the girls sitting around me.

Funny thing about Mr. Thomas, he could get mad at you but still be your friend. It was kind of scary at first. One minute he would be mad at you, his voice rattling the windows. The next minute he would be cracking one of the million silly jokes he knew. It took me awhile, but I figured out he only got mad at what I did, he wasn't really mad at me.

Sometimes he wouldn't even get mad, which was almost worse.

Once, Amy Fredricks, the girl I did **NOT** ask out for a date, was working on her math while Mr. Thomas was teaching reading.

"Whenever you are reading, it's important to try to figure out what is going to happen next. The author always gives you clues if you are paying attention." Mr. Thomas stated this bit of wisdom as he walked around the outside of the desks. I looked at his tie, the same fish one he had been wearing every day of school. I wondered if he had a bunch of the same kind or just one very tired tie.

Amy glanced over the notebook she had set up to conceal her math. She smiled at Mr. Thomas to show she was paying attention.

"Cause and effect, every story is built on cause and effect. Something happens and then something else happens because of what happened first, which was, of course caused by whatever it was that happened before it. Is that clear?" He continued his circling of the class as I tried to figure out what he had just said. I looked across the class at Stinky who shrugged his shoulders.

Amy, though, didn't notice because she was finishing up the twenty-fifth and final math problem.

Mr. Thomas kept talking.

"No event in a story stands alone. Everything is related to something else. A story is a lot like falling down steps. You must at least pass every step before you reach the conclusion of the stairs. Cause and effect."

Those of us who were really paying attention noticed he was watching Amy the whole time he walked. He came up behind her just as she finished the last problem. Closing her math book, she was ready to give her undivided attention to reading.

Mr. Thomas reached down and gently placed his hand in the center of the math paper. There was a soft crumpling sound that echoed off the classroom walls. We all watched as he lifted the paper from Amy's desk. Smiling at Amy, he continued talking as he wadded the math assignment into a little ball. Then he turned and made a perfect shot into the garbage can.

"Cause and effect."

Minutes later the reading assignment was given. Nothing was ever said about Amy's paper, but we all learned a lot from it. Amy was in shock for ten minutes and missed the assignment. She had to ask ME what it was, and then SHE got in trouble for talking in class! The assignment was, of course, on cause and effect.

Chapter 6
ONE SMALL JUMP

"Hey, guys, look at me!"

We turned to see Stinky hanging by his toes from the monkey bars.

"My cousin Sarah Elizabeth said I'm going to be really tall if I keep stretching myself like this."

"Isn't Sarah Elizabeth the one who told you to put sand in your bed if you want to trick the Sandman into letting you stay up late?"

"Yeah, it really worked to, I... Whoa!!!"

Stinky plummeted to the ground and landed on his head. He slips and falls on his head more than he probably ought to, which probably explains why Stinky is the way he is.

Stinky grew before any of the rest of us. He loved to rub it in too. He would leap high above us to catch a ball or reach up to erase the part of the chalkboard we had to jump to get. If you were a short kid like me, it kind of made you want to sock him in the kneecap.

One day at lunch Tim said, "Hey, you know what I saw today? I saw a fourth grader actually reach up and touch the top of the doorframe. He just reached up and touched it!"

The table became suddenly quiet. In those few words Tim had turned the simple act of touching the top of the door into a dream.

"Heck, if I keep hanging by my toes and keep growing, I'll be able to jump and touch it before Christmas," bragged Stinky.

"You keep falling from the monkey bars and that lump on your head will touch the top of the door!" chuckled Tim.

"I'll be in sixth grade before I'm able to do it unless you guys all get together and throw me," I said.

Stinky said, "I'm going to be the first third grader, after all I'm already taller than the rest of you guys."

Tim was the first to try though. Tim is the kind of kid who is always trying to impress the teacher and never gets in trouble. The next day he and Mr. Thomas were walking in front of the line on the way back from lunch talking about the fish tie.

"I've had this tie for 18 years," said Mr. Thomas. "It was a prize in a fishing contest."

"Is that the only tie you have?" asked Tim.

"I've thought about buying a new one, but this one has something special no other tie has."

Amy nudged me, "Yeah, that tie has a ketchup spot on it."

I chuckled, but I liked the tie too. It had become an old friend, something you could count on being there every day.

When Tim got to the door, he leaped and tried to touch the doorframe. He missed by several inches.

"Do you know what would have happened if you would have actually touched the top of the door?" Mr. Thomas asked Tim.

"No, what?" replied Tim, the smile vanishing from his face.

"You would have been given your choice of jumping to touch the top of the door 100 times without missing or writing one hundred times 'I will not jump while in line because I could possibly land on another student or the teacher.' "

There was a short pause as Tim's life passed in front of his eyes.

"What happens if you pick jumping and miss?"

Mr. Thomas smiled, "You get to start over."

Tim wasted no time telling us about the jumping. "Hey, guys, you aren't gonna believe what happens if Mr. Thomas sees you jumping!" We all huddled around him.

"Wait a minute, let's get Stinky. He'll want to know about this." I said.

"Stinky's at the dentist. He left right in the middle of math. We'll have to tell him later." Later never came.

The next day on the way back from lunch, Stinky and Mr. Thomas were walking side-by-side as they neared the doorframe.

Stinky tugged at Mr. Thomas' sleeve to make sure he was watching, "Hey, Mr. Thomas, watch this!"

"Stinky, no!" I whispered, but it was too late. Stinky gathered all of his 56 inches and hurled himself into the air.

Everyone stopped, breath held, hearts pounding, watching to see if Stinky's fingers would actually touch the doorframe. Mr. Thomas watched too, a small smile on his face and a look of disbelief in his eyes. For a moment I didn't think Stinky would make it, but he put that extra bit of effort into the leap. He knew everyone was watching, and Mr. Thomas always said to put that extra effort into everything you do. He wanted Mr. Thomas to be proud of him.

Stinky flung his hand towards the frame, and with a grunt, became the first third grader to touch the top of the door.

Most of us touched the top sometime during the year, but none of us did it with Mr. Thomas watching except Stinky and me. Stinky was the only one who stayed after school trying to touch the top of the door one hundred times without missing. Mr. Thomas graded math papers and Stinky jumped and counted.

"One...two...three...four...five...Darn, missed! One...two... three...four...five...six... seven...doggone it! One..."

After 15 minutes Stinky gave up and wrote the sentences.

Chapter 7
R-E-S-T-A-D-I-C-T-I-O-N-A-R-Y

"Work is good for you," intoned Mr. Thomas. "It keeps you awake, keeps you learning, and keeps you from goofing around."

"Keeps us from having any fun," whispered Stinky to Tim.

"Take out your math book, please, and a piece of paper."

From the beginning of the year until we got our first report card, Mr. Thomas gave us a ton of work every day. If we weren't doing math, we were doing spelling. If we weren't doing spelling, we were doing English. If we weren't doing...well, you get the idea. We were busy all the time. There was never a spare moment to draw or play games or anything.

Mr. Thomas loved to have us write sentences. I have to admit I wasn't very good at sentences when I started third grade, but in two weeks I was a pro. I could make sentences out of any list of words you could find, and do it quickly too.

Of course thinking of a sentence and spelling all the words right are two different things. Whenever we hit a word we didn't know how to spell, we would ask Mr. Thomas. He would sit, wisely stroking his beard, and do one of two things. He might tell you the word right away, which was the best. If he was busy that is what would usually happen. However, if he were sitting all alone with a little smile on his face, you would have to work to get the word.

"How do you think you spell 'rhinoceros', Mike?" was his usual opening question.

"I don't know. That's why I asked you." I said that the first time I wanted to know how to spell a word. Boy, did I get in trouble! I never made that mistake again.

"I'm sure you know how to spell part of it," he would say. "What's the first letter?"

"R."

Mr. Thomas would write the letter down on a scrap of paper.

"The second letter?"

"I."

His pen didn't move - a clue that I was wrong. It could take five minutes to pry a spelling out of Mr. Thomas if he was in one of his teaching moods. But, in the long run, you would get the word.

About five weeks into the school year a dictionary appeared on Mr. Thomas' desk. Then, when you wanted to know how to spell a word, the two of you would look it up together in the dictionary. The whole time he was turning pages, Mr. Thomas would be telling you about guidewords and the alphabet and stuff like that. I usually didn't listen and neither did anyone else, except Tim and the Kluggy twins. We would just quietly wait until he found the word.

Just after the first report card went home, Mr. Thomas changed. Whenever you asked how to spell a word, he would say, "Have you looked in the dictionary?"

"How can I find it in the dictionary if I don't know how to spell it?" demanded Tim one day, fifteen minutes before school was out.

"What are the first three letters of 'because', Tim?"

"B-e-c, that part's easy. I don't know if it's a-u or u-a next," Tim said impatiently. He really didn't want homework because he had piano lessons, soccer practice, and a couple of TV shows he wanted to watch.

Mr. Thomas was calm in the face of the storm, "If you know the first three letters and can recognize the word when you see it, you can find it in the dictionary. Give it a try."

With a glance towards the clock, Tim walked to the dictionaries to look up "because". He had wasted five minutes.

One other time Amy Fredricks, the girl with the pretty long black hair who sits behind me, walked to Mr. Thomas' desk. She picked a time when he was busy checking reading tests.

"How do you spell 'restaurant'?" she asked innocently.

Mr. Thomas didn't even raise his head, "R-e-s-t-a d-i-c-t-i-o-n-a-r-y." Amy frantically copied the letters down on her paper.

She was delighted. She had gotten the word without any trouble at all.

"Thanks!" she bubbled.

As she turned to leave, Mr. Thomas looked up with that little smile on his face and said, "Look closely at what you've written down."

Three kids, myself included, crowded around Amy and looked at what she had written. We all started chuckling at Mr. Thomas' joke.

"Oh, you!" Amy stomped off to the dictionaries.

Later, Mr. Thomas did give us a break from the dictionaries. He would offer us a choice: look the word up or write it twenty-five times. Sometimes writing was the quickest way.

By Christmas vacation, I was a whiz at dictionaries. I couldn't wait until Mr. Thomas started to teach us how to use a dictionary.

Chapter 8
THE PHANTOM TEACHER

"Halloween is great! You get to dress up crazy, get candy, and look at all the scary stuff in the stores. I mean, look at that skeleton! Halloween's my favorite holiday!" We were walking around a department store.

Stinky said, "It's not even a holiday. We don't get a day off from school, do we? I do like the candy though." He pulled a really nasty looking green face over his own.

"I don't care. It's still my favorite. I like it better than Christmas."

About three weeks before Halloween, I started planning my costume. Third grade is the last year we get to put on our costumes at school so I think it is important to have a good one.

Stinky said he was going to be a hobo. He's been a hobo ever since kindergarten and is pretty good at it. Tim found a really disgusting mask with green skin and fake blood running down the side. He put it on and pulled his father's old coat over his ears so only the mask showed. When I asked him what he was supposed to be, he said, "Ugly."

I felt they were taking the easy way out. A Halloween costume should be thought about; it should be carefully put together. It should have a good reason for being chosen besides being ugly or easy.

Usually I went as someone really important. I always found out all I could about the person before I made the costume. I would ask questions and, once I learned to read, I read books.

When I was in kindergarten I dressed up as Egbert the Chuckling Chicken. Egbert had his own TV show every day. He would sing and teach me not to hit other kids. (He never said a word about pouring milk on other kids!) I learned most of the basic rules of life watching Egbert and his Barnyard Buddies. That year I dressed in a chicken suit and walked around saying, "Bawk, bawk, remember, boys and girls, always be a good egg!" All the kids said I sounded just like Egbert.

During the summer between kindergarten and first grade, my family went on vacation to Springfield, IL. We saw where Abraham Lincoln was buried, where he had lived, and even went through his house. That year I decided to be Abraham Lincoln for Halloween. I looked through all the stuff we had picked up when we were in Springfield and studied the T-shirt I had gotten with his picture on it. I made a black top hat using a coffee can, some cardboard, and black paint. That year I walked around saying, "Four score and seven years ago," whatever that meant. I knew Lincoln had said it because it was on my T-shirt. Everyone called me Mr. President and said I sounded just like Lincoln.

Between first and second grade my parents took me camping in the Rocky Mountains. In the middle of the night a bear sniffed around our tent looking for something to eat. It was scary! A lady park ranger named Pam Rogers chased the bear out of the campground by yelling and banging trashcan lids together. I figured she deserved to be my Halloween costume for saving my life. So that year I went as Ranger Pam. I walked around banging lids together because my dad wouldn't let me say what Ranger Pam had said when she was chasing the bear. All the kids liked the bear story, but they told me the lids were giving them a headache.

As Halloween got closer my third grade costume was falling into place. I had decided to go as a person who was everything I ever wanted to be when I grew up: smart, talented, and rich because he was a teacher. I decided to be Mr. Thomas. I planned to shave the top of my head but leave some hair around the sides. I bought a fake beard at the store. At a garage sale I found a pair of glasses that looked just like Mr. Thomas'. Mom took the glass out of them so I wouldn't ruin my eyes. Luckily my dad had a fish tie. I took a piece of wood and made a guitar to show the talented part of Mr. Thomas. The only thing I didn't have was what I was going to say. I started paying close attention to Mr. Thomas to see if he said anything over and over.

The first thing I noticed he seemed to say a lot was "Mike Chappel, turn around and get to work." Another phrase Mr. Thomas said was, "I see a lot of people wasting time." The closer Halloween came, the more he said it. I had found my phrase!

I started to practice. I would stand in front of the mirror, lower my voice, and say, "I see a lot of people wasting time." The words rolled around in my mouth and came out firm and strong. I felt the power of those words as I imagined kids scurrying for their seats and pencils being moved noisily across the paper. "I see a lot of people wasting time." What a line! Maybe even better than, "Bawk, bawk, remember, boys and girls, always be a good egg." I practiced for hours.

The day before Halloween Mr. Thomas said, "Boy and girls, I have to talk to the principal in the hall for a second. You keep on working, I'll be right outside the door."

He hadn't been gone five seconds when Stinky turned around to talk to Tim. Amy and Carrie Hill started to give each other answers on the math assignment. Work stopped. School went on vacation until Mr. Thomas came back into the room. I looked around and saw what Mr. Thomas would have seen: kids wasting time! I knew what I had to do. I lowered my voice, and in a slow, steady tone, said, "I see a lot of people wasting time."

The room froze. Heads spun to look at the door so quickly I thought they might fall off their necks. Pencils started moving, trying to make up for lost time. The room became deathly quiet as everybody tried to figure out how Mr. Thomas could leave the room and still be there. Halloween had come to the third grade in the form of a voice without a body, a ghost in the corner: the Phantom Teacher!

Mr. Thomas chose that moment to come back into the room. He smiled at how hard everyone was working and was noticeably impressed.

"You know," he said, "there are three ways to control a class. The first is by the teacher being mean and nasty. The second is to assign a lot of work. The third is for the class to control themselves and not waste work time. I'm proud of you, you picked the right one!"

He smiled again and sat down. All the kids kept on working. Little did Mr. Thomas know there was a fourth way to control a class: the Phantom Teacher!

On Halloween I decided not to say, "I see a lot of people wasting time." I was enjoying watching everyone search the room for the way Mr. Thomas had talked without being there. I also thought they might get mad at me. I choose instead, "There are four ways to control a class." Everyone kept correcting me. I just smiled, tugged on my fake beard, and flicked my fish tie at them.

Chapter 9
TIME OFF FOR GOOD BEHAVIOR

Getting sick was always one of the fun parts of second grade. I'd get up in the morning and fake a few coughs. Mom would ask if I was OK, and I'd say I wasn't feeling very well. Usually I would spend the day watching TV or playing video games. Being sick was like a little vacation; time off for good behavior. No schoolwork, no teachers, and a decent lunch.

About a week after Halloween, I decided I'd worked hard enough to earn a day off.

I got out of bed and coughed. "Mom, I don't feel very good." Mom stuck a thermometer in my mouth and then left the room. While she was gone I rolled the thermometer around in my hands to warm it up.

"Oh, my," she said when she had returned and pulled the thermometer out of my mouth.

The day was great! I slept an extra hour and had a relaxing breakfast in front of the TV watching Egbert. Then I zapped about a zillion space aliens on my video games, read a new comic book, and took a nap. Mom fixed me grilled cheese for lunch. The rest of the day was about the same: TV, comics, and games. I chuckled as I noticed school was about to let out. I had missed all that work.

The next day I told Mom I felt well enough to go to school. She took my temperature and said I was normal, and then she chuckled.

I met Stinky at the edge of the playground. He was dragging his backpack.

"Boy, you sure were lucky you missed yesterday! Mr. Thomas gave us a ton of work. I didn't get it done until 8:00 last night." He gave his backpack a kick. "I've got more books in here than I've got in my desk."

Stinky went to the restroom when we got into the building, so I walked to class alone. I met Amy by the water fountain.

"So, how was class yesterday? Did you have a lot of work?" I asked.

Amy looked at me with her deep, green eyes, "Boy, we sure did. Mr. Thomas let me get your homework together. I set it on your desk."

My mouth dropped open, "Homework? What homework? I was sick yesterday. How could I have homework?"

"Mr. Thomas said that even though we get sick, we still have to do our work. He said if **he** gets sick, he still has to check papers and stuff," she paused, "I asked if I could get the work for you. Tim wanted to, but Mr. Thomas said I could do it." She smiled at me. When she smiles her eyes sparkle…not that I notice or anything.

Sure enough there was a neat stack of books and papers on my desk. A piece of paper with a yellow happy face on it listing all the assignments stuck out of the top book. Mr. Thomas must have noticed my surprise because he called me to his desk.

"Don't worry, Mike. I don't expect you to do that work today."

I gave a sigh of relief. Mr. Thomas had come to his senses. Of course he didn't expect me to do it.

"Thanks, Mr. Thomas. I don't think I'd ever get through it all."

Mr. Thomas smiled, "Just bring it in tomorrow morning."

I walked back to my seat and stared at the stack of books.

"See, I told you so," whispered Amy from behind me.

So all day I worked my hand to the bone trying to finish my work so I would have all night to do yesterday's work. I didn't get it done until 9:30. I think I fell asleep at my desk at home because I don't remember ever going to bed. I woke up wearing the same clothes.

That morning Mom said, "You look a little tired. I hope you're not getting sick again. Maybe you should stay home and rest."

I almost choked on my toast. "No, I feel fine. I don't ever want to miss school again."

I haven't missed a day since. Don't intend to either!

Chapter 10
THE MOONLIGHT SKATE

My school has a special night at the roller skating rink. It's a pretty neat deal because all us kids get to go skating on a school night, and our school gets part of the money to buy library books.

My Skate Night usually goes something like this: rent skates and try to get them on; stand up and immediately fall down (not everyone does this); go out on the skating floor and go around twice. If I do all those things, Mom lets me do whatever I want for the rest of the night. So I play video games, fall down a lot, bug her for candy, and do Shoot-the-Duck.

Shoot-the-Duck is where you go as fast as you can, squat down, and lift one leg off the floor. If you are the last one rolling, you win a prize. I've never won, but I'm getting better. Amy wins all the time. She's great on skates!

I always do Shoot-the-Duck for Mr. Thomas. He once told me he admires the people who try even more than those who always win. So I always try.

Most teachers don't come to Skate Night, but Mr. Thomas almost always comes. He doesn't skate. He just leans on the wall and watches us skate. He says he likes to see us fall down. Sometimes parents go over and talk with him, but he spends most of his time talking with kids. It's a good time to actually talk to Mr. Thomas because he says he doesn't have to wear his teacher hat at the skating rink.

"You going to Skate Night tonight?" asked Stinky at lunch.

"Maybe," I said.

"I couldn't go last time," Tim said through a mouthful of peanut butter and jelly. "What's it like?"

"It's really neat," bubbled Amy. "There's Shoot-the-Duck and the Moonlight Skate!"

"What's a Moonlight Skate?" asked Tim.

Stinky groaned, "It's not for us, it's for the old kids. They turn on a ball that hangs in the middle of the ceiling and then turn off the rest of the lights. The ball sends little spots of light all over the place. I think it's supposed to be romantic. You're supposed to hold your girl friend's hand and skate."

Milk squirted out of Tim's nose, "You're kidding! People actually do that? You'll never catch me doing it." We all nodded our agreement.

At the November Skate Night everything was going as usual. I had fallen down several times, lost at Shoot-the-Duck for Mr.Thomas, watched Amy win Shoot-the-Duck, talked with Mr. Thomas, and beat Stinky at the video games.

Stinky, Tim, and I started bugging the girls. We'd chase them around until they hid in the girls' restroom. We would hide until they came out, then we'd chase them again. It kept us busy for fifteen minutes or so. Then Tim and Stinky went to play video games, and I went to talk to Mr. Thomas again. Amy was already there. When I skated up, both of them turned to look at me.

"Hi," Amy said softly, and then she looked at Mr. Thomas. He gave a little nod of his head and turned to look at the skating rink. The lights dimmed and the ball came on. Little splashes of light swirled around the room and across Amy's face. She turned to look at Mr. Thomas again as, hand-in-hand, couples started to go out on the floor.

"Why not?" asked Mr. Thomas.

Amy turned to me, and with determination in her voice, said, "Do you want to Moonlight Skate with me?"

I felt a flash of heat in my face. I knew I was blushing. Good thing it was dark!

The problem was I wanted to moonlight with Amy and, at the same time, I was scared! What if someone saw me! Stinky and Tim would never let me hear the end of it. I looked at Mr. Thomas. I could see a little smile on his face as the light splashes bounced off his nose and hair.

"I won't even tell my cat," he said.

I looked at Amy - she was just standing there looking at me. I took one last look at Mr. Thomas and grabbed Amy's hand. We went out onto the floor and skated - two third graders in a sea of old kids.

We didn't talk as we skated around the first time. When we skated past Mr. Thomas, he gave us the thumbs-up sign. We waved back.

"Thanks for skating with me, I was afraid you'd say no," Amy said as we started our second lap.

"I kind of wanted to anyway. But I would never have been brave enough to ask you." I looked around nervously. "I sure hope nobody sees us!"

I felt proud to be skating with her and somehow taller and grown-up. I hoped my hand wasn't sweating.

When the song was over, Amy and I split up before the lights came on again. She went out one exit. I went out the other. We both got to Mr. Thomas at the same time.

"I don't think anyone saw you. They were all over at the games." He looked at both of us. "You looked good out there."

"You won't tell, will you?" I asked.

"I promised I wouldn't. I try very hard never to break a promise."

So... no one knew. Amy and I had moonlighted, and no one knew. No one kidded me. No one thought it was neat. I wanted to tell everyone. I wanted no one to know. It was horrible.

The next day I was thinking of how it felt to be skating with Amy as I walked through the door on the way back from lunch. I leaped in the air and felt my fingertips touch the doorframe.

I was the second third grader to touch the top of the door.

After school, Mr. Thomas and I stood alone in the doorway.

"Well, what's your choice?" he said.

I looked at the top of the doorway, so very far above me. I raised my hand to see how far it was from the top. It was a very long way.

"So, what do I have to write?" I asked.

Chapter 11
CUTE DOESN'T WORK ANYMORE

Carrie Hill walked into her first grade class and flipped her long brown hair from one side of her head to the other. Everyone turned to look at her. Then she smiled. A hush fell over the class, her smile brightened the far reaches of the room. Everyone smiled back, even the teacher. Carrie was very cute and a professional smiler. She had learned to use that smile the way a professional wrestler uses a body slam.

I first noticed how well she used that smile a week or so later. Jerry Kluggy was sitting at his desk, minding his own business, trying to make the car he was painting look like a car.

Smack! Carrie nailed him in the face with her paint smock for no reason. Jerry ran over to Mrs. Franklin, the art teacher.

"Mrs. Franklin, Carrie hit me in the face!" Jerry blurted. Mrs. Franklin put her hand on Jerry's shoulder and pulled him close.

"Did you do something to make her hit you?"

"No, Mrs. Franklin, I was just sitting there, and she hit me with her paint smock. See!" He pointed at the button scratch across his nose.

Mrs. Franklin looked over towards Carrie. She was sitting at her desk, wearing her smock, and painting a flower under the rainbow she had painted. You could almost see the halo over her head.

"Are you sure you didn't hit her first?" Mrs. Franklin looked sternly at Jerry. He looked down and nodded his head. He was confused.

"Carrie, would you come here, please?"

Carrie walked over to Mrs. Franklin's desk. She ignored Jerry altogether and flashed a cute-as-a-button smile at Mrs. Franklin.

"Carrie, Jerry says you hit him with your paint smock. Is that true?" Mrs. Franklin looked her square in the eyes.

"I didn't hit him. He's just mad because my rainbow is better than his stupid car." Carrie looked at Jerry and then back at the teacher. Then she turned on her smile again. "He said he was going to tell on me, but I didn't do anything!"

"Jerry, I'm surprised at you. You shouldn't make up stories about other people. Now apologize to Carrie and go back to your seat."

Jerry was in shock. Twice Carrie had hit him: once with the smock and once with her smile.

We watched Carrie get away with murder all the way through first and second grade. She would smile, flip her long, brown hair, and lie her teeth out. The teachers almost always believed her. She could talk a teacher, or anyone else for that matter, into letting her do almost anything just by turning on her smile and asking politely.

Stinky once gave her a piece of chocolate cake from his lunch. He said he didn't even remember it happening. She smiled at him in the lunch line and, when she left, his cake was gone. It was like the sun came out from behind a cloud when she smiled - it blinded you for a second.

About four months into third grade, we discovered that Mr. Thomas believed the only time we got thirsty or had to go to the bathroom was before school, after school, or at recess. He didn't seem to realize that sometimes you just had to go, no matter what the clock said. Even if you did get out of class, you always went alone.

"Can I go to the bathroom?" I asked one day.

"I bet you know how," Mr. Thomas replied. He had me confused, of course I knew how.

"Can I?" I asked again, beginning to hop up and down on one foot.

"Probably," he said seriously as he returned to checking English papers.

"Does that mean I can go?" The hopping was getting higher, and I was holding my knees together as hard as I could.

"Do you want permission, or do you want to know if you know how?" He smiled at me.

I was almost to the point where it didn't matter anymore. My knees were starting to cross. "Can I go to the bathroom, please?" I asked through gritted teeth.

"If you want permission ask 'May I," if you want to know if I think you know how say, 'Can I'."

I gave him a blank look. I couldn't believe it. My teeth were turning yellow, and he was giving me an English lesson.

I unclenched my teeth, "May I please go to the bathroom, please?" I hopped frantically up and down on one foot.

"Is it an emergency?" he asked without a hint of a smile but with a twinkle in his eye much unlike the panic in mine.

"Yes, but it won't be in a minute." I actually thought he might not let me.

"Well, I guess. Next time try to wait until recess."

I shot out of class, down the hall, and into the bathroom just in time.

One day Amy convinced Mr. Thomas to let her go to the restroom. She hadn't been out of the room thirty seconds when Carrie decided she wanted talk to Amy. She went up to Mr.

Thomas' desk. Stinky was already there talking about math.

"May I please go to the restroom?" she said in her sweetest voice. She flashed her award-winning smile and looked as cute as humanly possible. She was a real pro. I figured she'd be out the door in a second.

"No," Mr. Thomas smiled and went back to work trying to teach Stinky how to do a math problem with borrowing.

"But, Mr. Thomas, I really want to go." Sugar was dripping off her words. Her smile was so bright I thought I saw Stinky's skin start to tan. The water in Mr. Thomas' cup started to boil. She was using world-class cute. Stinky started to melt.

"No, Carrie."

"But, Mr. Thomas!" Her smile turned into the cutest pout I had ever seen.

"Carrie, I'm very busy trying to get Erving (Erving is what Mr. Thomas called Stinky.) to understand why it's impossible to take 8 away from 5. What part of 'no' did you not understand?" He stopped for a second in case Carrie had something to say. She didn't. "Anyway, I think you just want to go into the restroom and talk to Amy. You know I don't allow two people out of the classroom at the same time. No amount of cute is going to make me change my rules. Cute doesn't work in third grade, Carrie."

Carrie went back to her seat a changed person. Suddenly she realized that she was like everyone else. She would have to earn privileges just like everyone else. She would have to earn Mr. Thomas' respect by who she was and what she could do, not what she looked like or how well she smiled.

Even though Carrie's cute didn't work on Mr. Thomas, it sure worked on Stinky. He wobbled back to his desk and just stared at her for ten minutes with this lovesick look in his eyes. It was two days before Stinky could walk by her desk without breaking out in a sweat.

He never did understand why you couldn't take 8 away from 5. He just took Mr. Thomas' word that some things are simply impossible in third grade.

Chapter 12
HOMEWORK

The day after Thanksgiving Stinky lost his mind. I don't mean he went crazy or anything; he just stopped thinking, his brain went on vacation. The moment Stinky saw Santa Claus arrive in the parade on TV, he totally forgot about school. He was no longer interested in borrowing and carrying or reading or anything else that wasn't Christmas.

If there ever was a guy with sugarplums dancing in his head, it was Stinky. He watched Christmas specials on TV every night and spent hours working on his Christmas tree. He made lists and checked them twice; he stared at the packages under the tree and tried to guess what was in them. He is still the only kid I know who sent fourteen letters to Santa in one year.

With the help of his dad, he decorated the front of his house with red and white lights that blinked like a video game gone nuts. It was impossible to look at his house without getting dizzy.

Stinky REALLY liked Christmas.

The more Stinky thought about Christmas, the more he didn't think about school. Amy and I noticed the problem the second day back from Thanksgiving vacation. Fifteen minutes before school was out Mr. Thomas gave us a math assignment. Everybody panicked, the Kluggy twins looked like they were going to cry until Mr. Thomas said we could take it home for homework.

Stinky and I trudged down the steps and into the snow that covered the schoolyard.

"You ought to see our Christmas tree! It's bigger than I am, and it has all these lights on it...." He had told me about the same tree on the way to school that morning.

It wasn't until we got to my house that I was able to squeeze into the conversation, "You want to come in and do the homework?"

"I can't. My mom and I are going Christmas shopping," Stinky said, "I'll give you a call when we get back."

The call never came. I finished the math alone just before bedtime.

The next day, after attendance and the pledge, Mr. Thomas stood in front of the rows of desks.

"Please, pass your homework to the front," he announced.

We all started digging through our notebooks and slowly the math papers made their way to the front of the class. As the first person in each row handed him a stack of papers, Mr. Thomas counted them to make sure he had everyone's paper. He didn't say anything until he got to Stinky's row.

"I seem to be one short. Whose paper am I missing?" Mr. Thomas looked down the row of kids and then thumbed through the papers checking names. The class became quiet.

Suddenly a small, weak, somewhat squeaky voice cut through the silence, "I forgot mine at home."

All eyes searched for the voice. Mr. Thomas raised his head and looked directly at Stinky who did his best to crawl inside his desk.

"Erving, I'd like to talk to you at my desk. The rest of you may start writing sentences using the spelling words."

Mr. Thomas walked to his desk and sat down. Stinky didn't move.

"Erving," Mr. Thomas urged. Stinky later said walking to Mr. Thomas' desk that morning was the longest walk he had ever made. We all tried to look busy as we listened to Stinky say that he had left his math at home on his desk.

"I'll bring it in tomorrow, promise," Stinky was talking too fast like he always did when he was nervous. "I did it, really. I just left it on my desk."

"I didn't say you didn't do it, Erving, but the paper isn't here. It does neither of us any good on your desk. I would like you to stay in at recess and do the assignment over."

So while the rest of us played kickball, Stinky did his math. He was so upset; he didn't get his spelling sentences done. He took them home for homework.

That night Stinky and his mom made a couple million Christmas cookies. Stinky told me all about it as we walked to school, including all the crummy details and some samples.

Mr. Thomas asked for homework the moment everyone was in class, even before the pledge. Stinky walked up to Mr. Thomas' desk.

Looking at the floor, Stinky spoke quickly and softly, "I left my spelling sentences on the kitchen table last night and this morning my little sister dumped her cereal all over them." I think I saw his knees shaking.

"Well, that's another recess. This is two days in a row, Erving. Is there a problem I should know about?" Mr. Thomas had a concerned look on his face which was quite a bit different from Stinky's guilty one.

"No, honest, Mr. Thomas. My sister soaked them with milk when she reached for some toast! I didn't think you would want them if they were covered with frosted flakes."

Amy leaned forward and whispered, "I bet he didn't do it at all. I think he's lying."

"Nah, he wouldn't lie to Mr. Thomas. Stinky's smarter than that." I hoped I was right. Later Tim and I chased the Kluggy twins. Stinky did his spelling.

At the end of the day, Stinky still had homework. Three days in a row was a record in our class; nobody ever had that much homework.

The next morning Stinky didn't have his homework again, and Mr. Thomas was more than a little upset. Stinky said he had finished his English, and put it in his backpack. His backpack was still on the kitchen table.

Mr. Thomas spoke slowly and his voice was deeper than usual. "I want to believe you, Erving. But I think you are lying to me. This is the third time in three days that your homework isn't ready to turn in. Now, for the last time, and I want the truth, did you do your homework?"

Stinky gulped and took a deep breath. He was doing what no one else had ever done - he was not doing homework and kind of getting away with it. The world stood still as we waited for Stinky to find his voice.

"Erving, I'm waiting for an answer. If you didn't do your homework, it's best not to lie." His voice was slow and smooth. It had an edge to it that would have made me tell him I was the one who flushed the soap dispenser last week, and I wasn't even the one who did it!

Stinky swallowed hard and stepped off the cliff.

"It's in my backpack at home. I did it, I swear! I'll stay in and do it again if you want." Stinky was talking too fast again.

"Erving, I very much want to believe that you are not lying to me, but I'm having a hard time. Stand right there for a minute, please."

Mr. Thomas got up from his desk and walked quickly out of the room leaving Stinky standing in front of the class.

Usually when Mr. Thomas left the room I'd turn around and talk to Amy and Tim would talk to Stinky. Nobody moved or talked. I don't think I even breathed. We all just sat there listening to Stinky's heart going "thud, thud, thud."

When Mr. Thomas came back with Mr. Payson, the principal; Stinky's face turned white and the "thud, thud, thud" stopped altogether.

Mr. Thomas looked at us and said, "Mr. Payson is going to stay here with you while I take Erving home to get his backpack. Please, class, do page 49 in the math book. We'll be right back." The silence was heavy as Mr. Payson sat down at our teacher's desk. "Get your coat, Erving."

A hush fell over the class as we wondered if we would ever see Stinky alive again.

About twenty minutes later Mr. Thomas came back. Stinky didn't.

Mr. Payson returned to his office. Our teacher sat down at his desk and told us to do English page 52, the odd sentences.

Nothing was said for another hour. Mr. Thomas was very quiet and most of us were a little scared. I asked Mr. Thomas a question, and he answered softly. This wasn't the same guy who usually sat at the desk; this one was too quiet and just did his job. No jokes, no fun; just teaching.

The question we all wanted to ask, but no one dared, was, "Where is Stinky?" He didn't even come to lunch. The day lasted forever. I almost felt I had been robbed of a fun day of school.

When school was out, I saw Stinky slip out of the office. His head was down, and it was plain he didn't want to talk with anyone. I ran up to him and fell into step.

"Hey, what happened? Where've you been?" The words tumbled out of my mouth like fish over a waterfall. "I was worried about you. Tim thought Mr. Thomas left you at home."

"I was in the office. I had to sit in the office all day."

"Why? Couldn't you find your backpack?"

Stinky stopped and sighed. "Mr. Thomas drove me home and I ran in and got my backpack. As we drove back to school, he told me to get the homework out. I looked but it wasn't there. I told him I must have left it on my desk. Then Mr. Thomas turned around and drove me back home so I could get it off my desk. Except it wasn't there."

"Where was it? You did do it, didn't you?"

There was a long silence. "No, I never did it. I didn't have time to do it last night because *How the Grinch Stole Christmas* was on TV. I wanted to watch it. I thought Mr. Thomas would just make me stay in at recess again. That's what he always did before."

"You lied to Mr. Thomas? Wow! Why didn't you just tell him you didn't do it?"

"I never in a million years thought he'd drive me home. I'm grounded for two weeks at home, and I don't get recess until after Christmas. Mr. Thomas is mad at me too."

"He barely said anything when he got back. I'm not sure he even smiled."

Stinky and I walked the rest of the way home in silence.

I learned a lot that day. I learned never to lie about my homework. It's better to say I didn't do it and take my punishment. I learned that even Mr. Thomas has a hard time controlling himself sometimes, and he does it by being very quiet. I also learned that Mr. Thomas was more upset about being lied to by someone he had trusted than an unfinished homework assignment.

I also learned that Christmas presents could disappear from under a Christmas tree because Stinky lost three of his.

It was a long time before Stinky had homework again. It was even longer before Mr. Thomas trusted him again.

Chapter 13
CHOOSE CHRISTMAS PRESENTS CAREFULLY

"Why can't we get a Christmas tree?" I asked shoveling peas into my mouth.

"Honey, we're going to be in Florida for Christmas this year. We won't be home to enjoy it," said Mom.

"Oh, no! You mean we're going to stay with Aunt Lauri! I mean, I like her, but she always pulls my ears to see how big I've grown. And she always gives me a big, old slobbery kiss."

"She's my sister, you'll survive. It hasn't killed you yet," said Dad. "Do you want more mashed potatoes?"

It didn't seem like Christmas at all. No tree. No Stinky to play with at recess, and Aunt Lauri and her wet kiss to look forward to during vacation. I wondered if she kept pulling my ears if I'd be too big for my desk when I got back. Mr. Gregg wouldn't like that.

At least Christmas was coming to our classroom. Seems one of Mr. Thomas' traditions is to have a class gift exchange. Everybody writes his or her name on a slip of paper and drops it into a Santa hat. Then we pick out a name of someone to give a present to at the Christmas party. Everyone was really excited as they pulled a slip from the hat.

I closed my eyes as tight as I could. My hand felt around for the crumpled piece of paper that I had seen Stinky put into the hat. I grabbed one and looked at it: Jerry Kluggy. While Mr. Thomas was telling everyone that we couldn't trade names, I looked around for someone who wanted to trade.

Tim walked up to me at recess and said, "I got a girl! I don't know what to buy a girl!" He showed me his slip.

A light flashed in my head. "You want to trade? I got a boy."

"Sure! Anything's better than a girl." Tim danced away with Jeff Kluggy's name as I opened the piece of paper he had pressed into my hand - Amy Fredricks.

Mom said that since Mr. Thomas was such a good teacher, maybe I ought to get him a nice Christmas present. I thought it was a good idea for two reasons. First, I liked Mr. Thomas; and second, Mom was going to pay for it.

"Why don't we get him a coffee mug or a new fish tie? He drinks water all the time in class and he's been wearing the same tie with a fish on it for years," I suggested over breakfast.

"No, I'll get him something different," Mom said.

That left me all my money to buy something for Amy. What should I get her? I wanted something nice, but it couldn't be mushy. Maybe Tim had been right.

The last day before Christmas vacation Stinky came to recess.

"Hey, you got to come out!" I said running up to Stinky.

"Yeah, Mr. Thomas said it was an early Christmas present. I think Mr. Payson was sick of me being in his way."

As Stinky and I walked around outside, Stinky said, "Did you get Mr. Thomas a present? I got him a coffee mug that says, 'Number One Teacher' on it."

"I don't know what I got him. Mom picked it out and wrapped it before I saw what it was. I just hope he likes it." I had been so busy picking out the right gift for Amy, I'd forgotten about Mr. Thomas' gift. Luckily I had a good mom.

That afternoon we had our Christmas party. We had voted on who should be Mr. and Mrs. Santa Claus. They were the ones who got to pass out the presents. I liked that because I wasn't sure I could walk up and just hand a present to Amy. Stinky was chosen as Santa Claus; after all he was Mr. Christmas. Carrie Hill was chosen as Mrs. Claus. I thought that was funny because I knew that Stinky liked Carrie a lot. The class laughed as

Mr. Thomas put red stocking caps on Stinky and Carrie and got ready to take their picture.

"This will look great in the yearbook! Why don't you two hold hands?" Mr. Thomas smiled. I knew then that he had forgiven Stinky.

"No!" Carrie hid her hand behind her back. Stinky just stood there and blushed so red you couldn't tell where the hat stopped and his face began. The Kluggy twins were laughing so hard that Jeff fell on the floor.

After the picture was taken, Stinky and Carrie began to pass out the presents while we all drank red punch and stuffed Christmas cookies in our mouths. When the tree was empty we each had one present. Mr. Thomas had a pile.

"Open yours, Mr. Thomas!" said Tim. Mr. Thomas made Tim his secretary. While Mr. Thomas opened his presents, Tim wrote down what it was and whom it was from. Stinky's gift was the first to be opened. It was the coffee mug he had told me about. The second present was a mug, too, and so was the third. After fifteen minutes, Mr. Thomas had a new pen, four Christmas tree ornaments, six ties with different kinds of fish on them, several packages of cookies, and ten coffee mugs.

There were only two presents left. It didn't take a genius to figure out the one shaped like a cube was another coffee mug. Everyone laughed because it was a mug with a fish on it. My present was the last one Mr. Thomas opened. I hoped my mother hadn't picked out a coffee mug or tie like I had suggested.

Mr. Thomas pulled on his beard and said, "I hope it's another coffee mug. I'm starting a collection, you know. Of course, I could use a new tie as well." We all laughed as Mr. Thomas opened my gift.

When it was unwrapped, I wished that it had been a coffee mug. No one said anything. Stinky began to chuckle. Carrie giggled. Mr. Thomas just stared at it with that little smile on his face. He held it up high for everyone to see. It was a bottle shaped like a sleigh.

"What is it?" asked Tim, "I can't see."

"It's something that will last me a long time...aftershave lotion!" Mr. Thomas smiled and fluffed up his beard. "Thank you, Mike."

Stinky smirked, "Do people with beards use aftershave, Mr. Thomas?" Stinky was having a hard time controlling himself. He already knew the answer. The rest of the class began to get the joke and started laughing.

"My mom picked it out!" I shouted. "I *wanted* to get you a coffee mug, but she said, 'No, I'll get something different'!" I used a high momlike voice when I said what my mom had said.

Mr. Thomas was laughing then - the most I'd seen him laugh since Stinky's homework disaster. It felt good to see him laugh again. He later said that was the best present he got...his laugh.

Then we got to open our gifts. Stinky got a model car from Carrie, and Tim got a notebook from Jerry. Jeff Kluggy got five really neat pencils and a pen from Tim. Everyone liked his or her gifts a lot.

My gift was in a card. It was from Amy. She stared at me the whole time I was opening it. I wondered if she had traded for my name like I had for hers. I couldn't believe my eyes when I saw what it was: three free passes for the skating rink. The card said, "Maybe we could go together."

"What did you get?" asked Stinky.

I blushed, "Oh, just a couple of passes for the skating rink." I was watching Amy as she opened my gift to her. Her eyes opened wide when she saw that I had given her the same thing: three free passes to the skating rink.

We looked at each other for a second and then started talking to other kids.

Three days after Christmas I got home from Aunt Lauri's house. She had slobbered all over me and pulled my ears, but I had survived just like my dad said I would. I had a card in the mail from Mr. Thomas thanking me for my gift. He said he gave the aftershave to his father who would have been disappointed if someone hadn't given him aftershave lotion.

The next day I called up Stinky and asked if he wanted to go roller-skating. Then I called up Amy and told her that Stinky and I were going skating and why didn't she call up Carrie and come on out to the skating rink.

That afternoon was fun. Stinky and I chased Amy and Carrie around the skating rink. I fell down a lot, and Amy won at Shoot-the-Duck. When the Moonlight Skate came along, Amy and I held hands and skated. Stinky and Carrie watched us go around, laughing and pointing. But when we came back around the second time, they weren't standing on the side anymore.

"Look!" shouted Amy. When I looked ahead I saw Mr. and Mrs. Santa Claus skating hand-in-hand just in front of us.

"Hey, Stinky!" I hollered.

Stinky turned around, "Ho, ho, ho, Merry Christmas!" was all he said.

Chapter 14
THERE'S NO DAY LIKE A SNOW DAY

About the end of January we had a huge snowstorm. School was called off for two days because it was impossible to drive on the roads. Stinky and I played outside most of the time. We had snowball fights, went sledding over at Eureka Hill, and made an army of snowmen. We got wet and cold and had more fun than the time Tim's little brother sat on Tim's birthday cake.

About noon on the second day, Stinky and I went to visit Amy and Carrie. Amy had spent the night at Carrie's house. I had never been to Carrie's neighborhood, much less her house, so I was looking forward to the trip.

Stinky and I stumbled through the deep snow and turned onto Carrie's street. Stinky stopped and quickly ducked behind a bush in someone's yard.

"Look!" he whispered urgently. I followed his pointed glove and saw someone shoveling snow out of a driveway.

"So? What's so big about someone shoveling snow?"

"Can't you see who that is? It's Mr. Payson! I'd recognize his coat and hat anywhere. I had to sit next to that coat when I was in his office. That stupid hat was always falling off the coat rack right into the middle of my paper. I'd recognize that hat anywhere."

We hid behind the bush for a while watching Mr. Payson throw the snow from his driveway into the driveway next door.

"I didn't know Carrie lived next door to the principal," I said.

"Me, neither. You'd think Carrie would have told us." Stinky reached down and picked up a handful of snow and began to make a snowball.

Mr. Payson finished his driveway and began to scoop the sidewalk that ran in front of his house. He was coming towards us. Stinky continued to make a snowball as he watched Mr. Payson.

"Hey, what are you going to do with that snowball? That's the principal. You can't hit him with a snowball. He'd kick you out of school forever. You'd always be a third grader!"

There was a gleam in Stinky's eye and his jaw was set in determination. He wasn't staring at Mr. Payson; he was staring at the hat. It was a tall, brown hat, the kind old-time TV detectives wear. It seemed to be sitting loosely on his head.

Stinky kept his eye on the hat and whispered, "I bet I can knock that hat right off his head."

"What!" My jaw dropped open in disbelief. I stared at Stinky with wide eyes. "You know you aren't that good with a snowball. You hardly ever hit me when we have snowball fights. You'll miss him and the hat. Even worse, you'll miss and smack him."

The strength left Stinky's arms. They fell to his side. "You're right. I'm crummy with a snowball. But I hate that hat! Just once I'd like to see that ugly old brown thing get what's coming to it."

We were silent for a second. The only sound on the street was the scraping of Mr. Payson's shovel on the sidewalk.

Stinky moaned, "I wish I was as good as you with a snowball. You can hit anything."

"Well," I said, "I am pretty good. Remember that squirrel I hit the other day? He was so mad he sat up in a tree and chattered at us for ten minutes."

Stinky grabbed my arm, "I bet *you* could knock that hat off Mr. Payson. It's bigger than the squirrel, and closer, too!" Stinky was really warming up to the idea.

"Oh, no!" I held my hands up in front of me as if to block the idea. "I don't want to throw a snowball anywhere near the principal."

Stinky studied me for a second and then said, "You're right. You'd probably miss anyway."

"No, I could hit it. I just don't want to throw at the principal, that's all." I reached down and picked up a handful of snow.

"If you're that good, why don't you do it? If you're that good Mr. Payson won't even know his hat got knocked off. He'll think it was blown off by the wind."

"Yeah, maybe...." I looked at Mr. Payson. He was leaning against his snow shovel. He was a perfect target.

"I don't think you can do it! I dare you to do it. I'll even give you ten dollars from my Christmas money. Don't double-dare me either, because we both know I can't do it." Stinky dropped the snowball he'd been working on, leaving me the only one holding snow. "Come, on. I dare you!"

I hated things like this. Once, my oldest cousin wanted me to smoke a cigarette and had dared me. I turned that down because I knew smoking was dangerous. But this seemed different. This was just a snowball and a hat, a safe bet.

I studied Mr. Payson leaning on his shovel. His hat, sitting tall on his head, was an easy target. I glanced at Stinky. "Ten dollars?"

Stinky nodded. "Ten dollars when we get back to my house."

I looked at Mr. Payson. I knew he wouldn't lean on that shovel much longer. The door opened on the house next to Mt. Payson's and out stepped Carrie and Amy dressed in their winter coats and scarves, almost as if they were coming out to watch me knock that hat into the next town.

I studied the wind. There wasn't much. I looked around to see if anyone was watching us - no one. Amy and Carrie hadn't even seen us. I rounded the edges of the snowball I'd been working on, making sure it would fly straight and not get hung up on my glove.

Stepping from behind the bush, I took a deep breath and threw hard and straight. I threw the snowball so it would travel in a graceful arch as gravity pulled it down. I threw straight at Mr. Payson's hat. Then I stepped quickly behind the bush. Stinky and I watched as it sailed towards Mr. Payson.

"I didn't think you'd do it! Are you crazy? That's the principal!"

I looked at Stinky. I looked at the snowball. It seemed to have been flying for a long time. Everything seemed to be happening in slow motion. There was nothing I could do but watch. Carrie noticed the snowball and pointed it out to Amy.

There were three things I wanted to do then. I wanted to run; I wanted to yell, "Duck."; and I wanted to see if I actually hit the hat or nailed the principal in the back of the head.

I watched. Stinky watched. Amy and Carrie watched. The snowball homed in on Mr. Payson like a heat-seeking missile. I held my breath. Mr. Payson leaned on his shovel and looked at the two girls.

The snowball tipped the top of the hat, knocking it into the air. It gracefully tumbled onto the sidewalk, bounced once, and rolled into the snow.

"You did it!" yelled Stinky. "You knocked his hat off!" His voice echoed off the houses. I slapped my hand over his mouth before he could yell anything else… like my name.

Mr. Payson, hearing Stinky's voice, spun around and looked towards the bush. We ducked down and tried to disappear. I figured Mr. Payson would find us right away by just following the banging of my heart. He took a step towards us and looked around.

"He doesn't see us!" whispered Stinky. "Let's make a run for it. We can circle around and go in Carrie's back door."

"He'll see us if we move. He's going to kill us!" I watched as Mr. Payson moved closer to our bush. My heart continued to bang against my ribs. I was so scared I wasn't sure I could run.

"Well, I'm going!" Stinky hissed. "You do whatever you want, but I'm getting out of here." Stinky took off in a crouched run, hugging the bushes that led around the house. I watched him go, hesitated, and then took off after him.

We went around the house, running as hard as we could through the snowdrifts in Mr. Payson's back yard. When we got to the edge of his house, we stopped. We had to go across the open space between his house and Carrie's.

Stinky stuck his head around the corner of the house. "He's still looking around, he's down by the bush. Come on!"

We sprinted the short distance to Carrie's back porch. After pounding on the door for two or three weeks, Carrie's mom finally came to the door. She opened the door and we stepped into the kitchen - breathing hard and dripping snow all over the floor.

"Is Carrie home, Mrs. Hill?" Stinky asked in his most polite voice between gasps for breath.

"Why, no, she isn't, boys. She and Amy just went outside to build a snowman over at Amy's house. Was she expecting you?"

"No, we thought we would just stop by to see what she was doing." Stinky looked nervously out the door to see if Mr. Payson had followed our footprints. "Well, I guess we'll go now."

I edged for the door with Stinky right behind me. Before we went out, I looked around. Mr. Payson was nowhere in sight. When we finally stepped out, I heard the scrape on a shovel on the sidewalk. Mr. Payson was back at work!

We jumped off Carrie's porch and ran through the backyards, avoiding Mr. Payson. I was beginning to feel pretty good. I had knocked the hat off the principal and gotten away with it. Soon, I would be ten dollars richer; and when Stinky told everybody what I had done, I'd be a hero.

When we got to Stinky's house, he immediately went and got a ten-dollar bill. "Here," he said. "You earned it. What a throw! You just knocked that hat off as easy as anything. I can't wait to tell the guys!"

The next day we were back in school. Stinky had spread the word about my death-defying throw. Amy and Carrie had backed him up. I was cool. I was King for the day. Everyone wanted to eat lunch with me, and I was everybody's friend. I had never been so popular in my life.

About the middle of the afternoon, Mr. Payson appeared at the door to Mr. Thomas' room. My heart crawled up my throat, hid under my tongue, and began to beat harder than a drum in a rock and roll band. Mr. Payson talked with Mr. Thomas, occasionally glancing at me. Then he left. I was just about to relax when Mr. Thomas said, "Mike, could I see you at my desk, please?"

Since it was a question, I thought maybe I could say no, but decided instead to say nothing. I remembered what Stinky had said about the long walk to Mr. Thomas' desk when you knew you were in trouble. I felt all the eyes in the room watching as I walked the three miles across the room to the big, cluttered desk where Mr. Thomas sat.

"Mike, did you throw a snowball at Mr. Payson yesterday?" Mr. Thomas was trying to look serious, but he was having a hard time. A smile kept slipping through the frown. It made me feel a little better.

I looked at Mr. Thomas and then at my feet. My tongue seemed to have disappeared.

The class was quiet. I heard a pencil crash to the floor and a chair move as the owner bent to pick it up. I looked at Mr. Thomas again. He had lost his smile.

"Well?" he urged.

"Stinky dared me! He said he would give me ten dollars if I could knock the hat off! I didn't hit him, just the hat." I could hear Stinky gasp when he heard his name. I didn't want to get him in trouble but the words just came out. "I didn't want to do it. He dared me!"

Mr. Thomas stared at me for a long time as I twitched in my shoes.

"If Erving had dared you to jump off of a building, would you have done it? How about stepping in front of a moving train? How about if he dared you to take drugs or smoke, would you have done it?"

"No, that would be dumb. I could hurt myself. This was just a stupid snowball." I looked Mr. Thomas in the eye. Did he think I was an idiot?

"So, if it's dangerous for you, you won't do it. You have to think about other people, too. If that snowball would have hit Mr. Payson in the ear, he might have lost his hearing." Mr. Thomas was serious - he wasn't lecturing me - he was talking facts. I hadn't thought about missing, or about Mr. Payson. "You have to think of as many things that might happen before you do anything. Especially if it involves another person."

My head dropped again. I looked at the floor. He was right. I wanted to run away, but I knew I couldn't.

Mr. Thomas was quiet for a while.

"I'm glad you're a good shot. You're in trouble, but not as much as you could be if you had missed."

"What's going to happen to me? Is Mr. Payson going to kick me out of school?"

"Mr. Payson and I talked to your parents. Since this happened off the school grounds, it was up to your parents how we handled it. You're lucky; you've got good parents. They felt you should be punished, and they said we should do it at school since it involved Mr. Payson. Some parents would have ignored it, and you wouldn't have learned anything."

"So, what happens now?"

"You're going to miss a week of recess and stay after school for a week to do some chores."

"Thanks, Mr. Thomas. I really thought I'd be kicked out. I promise I'll never throw a snowball again."

"I won't take that promise, Mike. You're good at throwing. You might make a great pitcher someday. Just think about why you are throwing and what might happen. I would rather you promise never to take another dare. You might not be so lucky next time."

"I promise, Mr. Thomas." I really meant it too.

Chapter 15
MR. MOUSE

Mr. Thomas pulled on his beard as he looked at his class. He was wearing a tie with an owl on it. He had been rotating through the ten ties he had received for Christmas presents. He had done the same with the coffee mugs. "This is the last full day of school. We have to get the classroom ready for summer today. Anything we can do today will be one less thing I have to do tomorrow."

Amy, her long, black hair pulled back into a ponytail, raised her hand. "Mr. Thomas, did we all pass?"

The whole class froze as we waited for the answer to the last important question of third grade.

Mr. Thomas looked around the class. He looked at me, Mike Chappel, the kid who spent a week in the office for knocking the principal's hat off with a snowball. He looked at my best friend Stinky. Stinky was the only kid Mr. Thomas ever drove home to get homework only to find Stinky hadn't even started it. Stinky spent some time in the principal's office too. Then there was my girlfriend Amy, and Carrie, Stinky's girlfriend.

The class waited. Even the kids who were sure to pass, like Jeff and Jerry Kluggy or my friend Tim, were worried.

"You'll have to wait until tomorrow to find out for sure, but I will tell you one thing: at least one person in this room will not be going to fourth grade."

The news sat like a bomb in the middle of the floor. I felt like it was sitting on my desk. I looked at Stinky. He had the same bomb on his desk.

"But before anybody gets to go to fourth grade, we have to finish third grade. I need a couple more grades before I fill out the report cards tonight. I'm not going to assign a lot of work today, but what I do assign will be important." A sigh of relief ran through the class as Mr. Thomas wrote the assignments on the board.

The work wasn't that hard, and there really wasn't much of it. The hardest thing I saw on the board was clean out your desk and locker. I hadn't seen the back of my desk since January. I only saw it then because Mr. Gregg, the school janitor, had dumped it so he could make it bigger for me.

Amy poked me in the back with her pencil. "I hope you brought a big bag and a cage. I think there's something living in your desk." She giggled. Mr. Thomas glanced over at her.

"Everyone needs to get working on the math assignment. Mike, you start working on your desk. I think it might take you most of the day." The class laughed as they took out their math books.

"Does that mean I don't have to do the math?" I asked.

Mr. Thomas smiled, "No. If you want to do the math first, go ahead. I just thought you might want to do the hard stuff first."

I pushed and shoved papers and books around in my desk trying to find my math book. Maybe cleaning would be easier. I started to pull great handfuls of papers from my desk.

Amy picked up one of the papers from the floor. "This paper is from October! I thought you cleaned your desk when Mr. Gregg dumped it."

"No, I just stuffed the stuff back in it. Hey, look, here's that piece of candy Stinky gave us on his birthday!"

Stinky looked up, "That was in January, Mike."

Amy picked it up, "Yuck, it looks like it's been chewed on. Do you still want it?"

"Naw, just throw it away." I reached in and grabbed another handful of papers. "Hey, these look like they've been shredded."

Amy got down on her knees and started straightening papers as I pulled more and more things out of the desk. I had just pulled out my third handful of shredded paper when something shot past my arm and landed on Amy's back.

"A mouse!" shouted Stinky. The mouse leaped from Amy's back and took off across the floor.

"AAAAAAAA!" screamed Amy. She jumped up and ran the other direction across the floor.

The Kluggy twins jumped up on their chairs as the mouse scurried around the edge of the classroom.

"Stay calm!" shouted Mr. Thomas. "Everyone just stay in their seats. The mouse is trying to find a way out of the room."

"I'll get him," said Stinky. "I always catch the mice at home." He grabbed a garbage can and ran after the mouse. The rodent was having a nervous breakdown over by the bookshelf. With the possible exception of Amy, the mouse looked more shook up than anyone in class. Stinky walked slowly towards the bookshelf carrying the garbage can. The whole class got quiet.

Stinky got right next to the mouse and slowly started to lower the can. He was just six inches above the mouse when WHAM! He slammed the can down.

The class began to applaud, and Stinky took a bow.

"Good job, Erving. Now slide that big piece of cardboard under the can and take Mr. Mouse outside." Mr. Thomas patted him on the back.

"Be careful not to pinch his leg," said Carrie.

We all watched Stinky slowly slide the cardboard under the garbage can and lift it in the air. He started for the door.

"Can we go watch, Mr. Thomas?" asked Carrie flashing her award-winning smile. Carrie's smile always had a big effect on Stinky, and he almost dropped the can.

"Sure, why not? The mouse has probably been living in Mike's desk since Christmas vacation. He's as much a part of our class as anyone else."

We all followed Stinky down the hall, past the principal's office, and out the front door.

"I'll let him go over there by the bushes," said Stinky.

We watched as he set the cardboard and the can down on the lawn. He lifted the can straight up. Mr. Mouse sat still for a second and then shot into the bushes. We all cheered and patted Stinky on the back. Then Mr. Thomas took us to the playground and let us run around for a few minutes to celebrate Mr. Mouse's last day of school.

Amy caught me on the playground. "If I have to sit next to you next year, you better keep your desk clean! I don't ever want a mouse to jump on me again!"

Mr. Thomas came walking by just then. "Mike, don't you know you aren't supposed to have pets at school?"

Mr. Thomas and I laughed as the class lined up to go indoors.

Chapter 16
NOT EVERYONE GOES ON

The last day of school is always a little strange. For one thing, it's only one hour long. It always starts out looking weird as well. The room where we had spent the last nine months looked like an alien world. Mr. Thomas had taken everything down from the walls and ceiling. Everything was straightened, cleaned, or covered with newspaper to keep the summer school kids from messing with the books and supplies. Even Mr. Thomas' desk was clean. There were only two things on it: a coffee mug that said "Number One Teacher" and report cards.

When Stinky and I came into the room, Mr. Thomas was sitting at his desk just sort of staring off into space. It was the kind of stare that makes you be very quiet. We sat down without saying a word. Almost everyone else was there.

I stuck my hand in my desk to see if I had anything to play with while I waited for Mr. Thomas to start class. I found a little piece of shredded paper left over from Mr. Mouse's nest. I showed it to Stinky, he choked back a laugh. Amy snickered too.

Then I remembered what Mr. Thomas had said about the one person who would not be going to fourth grade. I shoved the paper into the desk. Maybe Mr. Thomas hadn't seen me acting like a little kid.

The silence was broken when Carrie raised her hand.

"Yes, Carrie," said Mr. Thomas.

"What are we going to do today?" she asked.

"I thought we'd daydream for awhile, then I'd pass out report cards, and we'd all go home."

"Who didn't pass, Mr. Thomas?" Tim couldn't hold the question in any longer.

Mr. Thomas looked at the clock; we still had forty-five minutes of school left. He stood up and walked to the front of the class. "So, you don't want to daydream anymore? Well, if that's what you want, we'll go back to the real world."

He smiled and looked around the room. He was wearing his old fish tie again, the first time since Christmas. "I said yesterday that one person will be not be going to fourth grade. Tim, what if it were you?"

Tim sat straight up in his chair. The bomb had landed on his desk. "What?" he croaked.

"If you are the person not going to fourth grade, and I'm not saying it is you, what would you do?"

"Probably never go home. My parents would kill me if I flunked."

"Do you think you did?" Mr. Thomas asked. "Think hard. You know how you did this year. Should I have held you back?"

Tim squirmed in his seat. "I think I passed. I don't read as well as I think I could, but I don't think I'm bad enough to flunk."

"Then next year, in fourth grade, you should work more on reading. You passed."

A big smile came over Tim's face. He pretended to melt into his chair. Stinky gave him a big thumbs-up sign.

"Everyone think. Did you pass? Think about whether you worked hard enough this year to go on. Think about whether you are able to control yourself enough to go on to fourth grade." As he talked, Mr. Thomas was passing out little pieces of paper and pencils. "On this piece of paper I would like you to put your name and whether or not you think you passed. Be honest with yourself. That doesn't mean be hard on yourself, just don't lie to yourself. When you are done, hold up the paper and I will collect it."

I looked at the piece of paper in front of me. I knew what I wanted it to say, but I wasn't sure if it should. This was hard! I looked over at Stinky. He was staring off into space. I looked at the clock, thirty-five minutes to go. I had to write something down.

I thought about the year. I thought about all the stupid things I had done. I also thought about how my report card had kept getting better. It wasn't as good as Tim's or Amy's, but I had gotten better. I wrote down "passed", folded the paper twice, and handed it to Mr.

Thomas when he walked by my desk. He read it and smiled. At least he didn't laugh.

When everyone had turned in their last assignment of third grade, Mr. Thomas picked up the report cards from his desk. I glanced at the clock, ten minutes to go.

"You were all correct. Everyone knew whether they should pass or not. I've found if you are honest with yourself, you aren't surprised very often."

"Who didn't pass, Mr. Thomas?" asked Stinky.

Mr. Thomas ignored him and began passing out the report cards. Everyone immediately looked at them. There on the bottom line I saw the words: "fourth grade"! I had really passed! I looked around the room. Everyone was smiling. Nobody looked sad.

"Remember," Mr. Thomas said, "What you got on your report card is your business. If you want to show someone your grades you may, but you have no right to ask anyone else about their grades."

"Mr. Thomas, who didn't pass?" demanded Stinky.

"Did you pass, Erving?" asked Mr. Thomas.

"Sure I did!" said Stinky.

"I did too," said Amy.

"Me, too," said the Kluggy twins together.

One by one everyone said that they had passed. I looked at the clock just as Mr. Thomas said, "It's been a good year. I've enjoyed being your teacher. Have a great summer."

He paused and glanced at everyone, looking right into his or her eyes. "In order to leave you must either shake my hand, get hugged, or both. Your choice."

We lined up and, one by one, filed past Mr. Thomas getting shook or hugged. Stinky and I were at the end of the line. Stinky chose the handshake. I took both. I was really going to miss Mr. Thomas. As Stinky and I left the room, I turned and said, "Who isn't going to fourth grade, Mr. Thomas?"

"Think about it, Mike. You'll figure it out." Then he winked and began to read a list of names that had been on his desk. We left the room, leaving him and his fish tie there alone.

THE END

Mike Anderson

About the Author

Mike Anderson is an award-winning storyteller, educator, writer, and entertainer. A collection of his short stories, *The Great Sled Race*, was awarded a 2000 Parents' Choice Silver Honor. Mike is also nationally renown, appearing at the National Mountain Music Festival, holding a prestigious position on the faculty of the Mountain Dulcimer Workshops at Appalachian State University, Boone, NC and West Carolina University, NC Dulcimer Workshops, as well as presenting workshops and concerts across the United States. Mike's children's concerts are very popular and his Early Childhood shows are legendary. He received a National Children's television award for a show he wrote and hosted. Under the auspices of the Illinois State Board of Education, Mike has conducted many teacher and parent workshops for developing literacy through the art of storytelling.

Visit him on the web at

http://www.dulcimerguy.com

Printed in the United States
19992LVS00001B/175-192